OLIVER AND GEORGE

For Judy and Lex, who have always treasured
good friends and good books.

First published in Australia 2014
This edition first published in 2020 by New Frontier Publishing Europe Ltd
Uncommon, 126 New King's Rd, London SW6 4LZ
www.newfrontierpublishing.co.uk

A CIP catalogue record for this book
is available from the British Library.
ISBN: 978-1-913639-34-1

Printed in China
10 9 8 7 6 5 4 3 2

OLIVER AND GEORGE

PETER CARNAVAS

NEW FRONTIER PUBLISHING

Oliver was ready to play

but George was busy.

'Finished yet?'
Oliver asked.

'In a minute,'
said George.

Oliver waited for a minute

but nothing happened.

So Oliver threw a paper plane at George.

George got **so mad** that he …

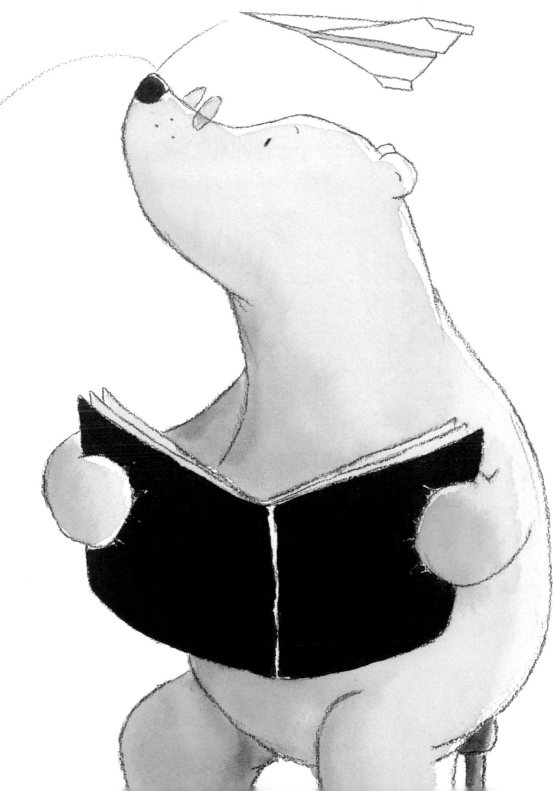

didn't do anything.

George wasn't mad at all.

Oliver broke George's chair.

George got **so mad** that he …

didn't do anything.

George wasn't mad at all.

Oliver tipped porridge on George's head.

George got **SO mad** that he ...

didn't do anything.
George wasn't mad at all.

So Oliver left George alone.

But not for long.

He pulled
George's ears.

He tickled George's nose.

Then Oliver snatched the book
from George!

Oliver said sorry
and so did George.

'Shall we play now?' asked George.
'Okay,' said Oliver.

'In a minute.'